The Pirates of SCURVY SANDS

To the west of SCURVY SANDS sank me ship with all its hands. I dragged me TREASURE CHESTS ashore, where they shall lie for evermore!

MAD JACK McMUDDLE

Who always got lost and was never quite sure of which oceans he'd crossed. 'Cause his map-reading skills went often awry, he'd a compass tattooed above his left eye.

Rats in yer bilges? King chopped off yer hand? Treasure lost its sparkle?

Then come to SCURVY SANDS!

Park yer ship in HERE

Dig for Mad Jack's GOLD!

Pedalos

A TEMPLAR BOOK

First published in the UK in 2018 by Templar Publishing,
an imprint of Kings Road Publishing, part of the Bonnier Publishing Group,
The Plaza, 535 King's Road, London, SW10 0SZ
www.templarco.co.uk
www.bonnierpublishing.com

Copyright © 2018 by Jonny Duddle

1 3 5 7 9 10 8 6 4 2

ISBN 978-1-78370-409-5

For the scurvy Capsticks, who dared to
holiday with PIRATES!

And...
For Tamlyn, Lisa, Mike and Cursed Kate,
who were press-ganged on a voyage that
they thought would never end...

This book was typeset in
Aunt Mildred and Tree.
The illustrations were sketched with
pencil and coloured digitally.
Designed by Mike Jolley
Edited by Kate Haworth

Printed in China

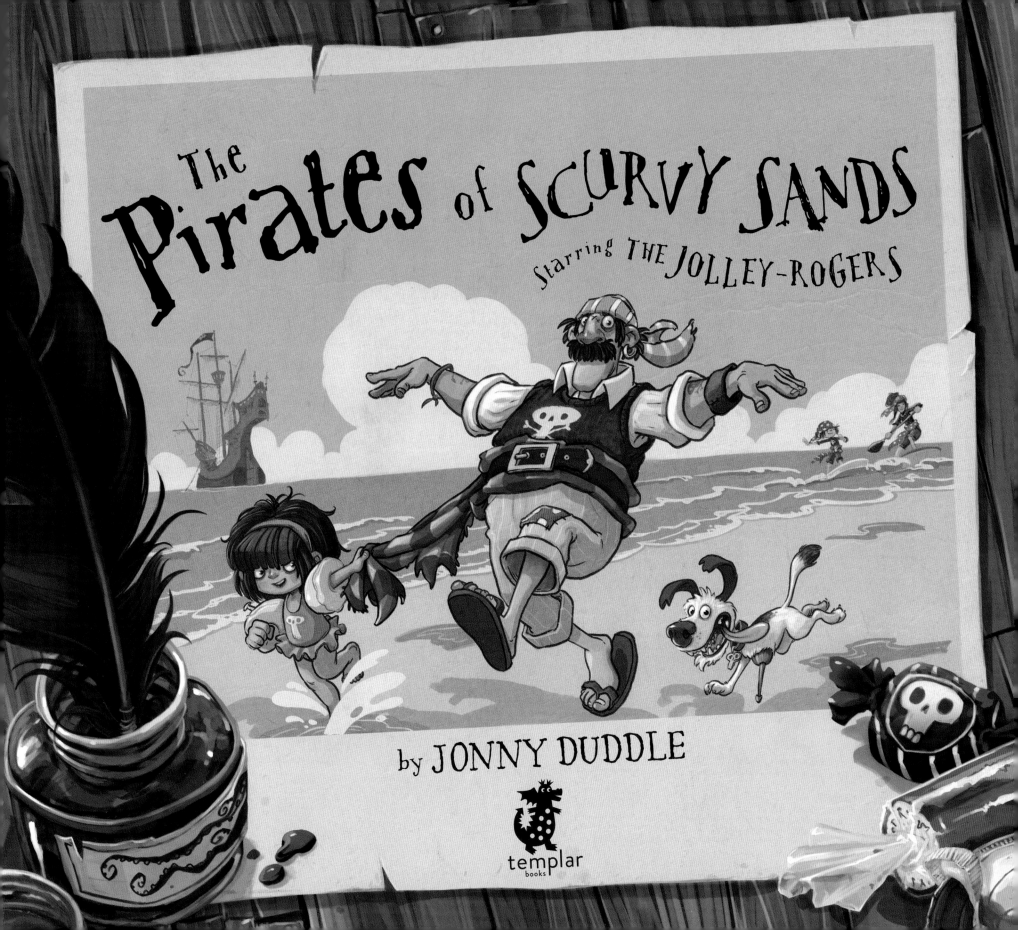

The Pirates of Scurvy Sands

starring THE JOLLEY-ROGERS

by JONNY DUDDLE

templar
books

Matilda lived in Dull-on-Sea, a charming seaside town. It's bleak in the midwinter...

...but in summer folk come down to frolic in the sea and play in the arcades,
to sizzle in the midday sun and dig with plastic spades.

Matilda had a penfriend,
who sailed the scurvy sea;
a pirate boy named JIM LAD,
he sent letters to the quay.

They arrived in old green bottles,
bunged up with a cork.
Jim didn't have a phone;
it was the ONLY way to talk.

Dear Tilly,

We're goin' on a voyage, a special pirate trip!
We'll pick you up tomorrow, you can come aboard our ship!
We'll be sailing through the darkness, a whisper in the night.
I'll see you shortly after dawn,
by the early morning light.

Love,   Jim Lad

xxx

SCURVY

Can I go to Scurvy Sands?

...Matilda asked her dad.

Oh... Erm... I suppose you could... Those pirates aren't so bad.

Matilda packed her swimsuit, some shorts and summer tops, her toothbrush, snorkel, suntan lotion and her NEW flip-flops.

At dawn, Matilda's parents took her to the harbour side, past the yachts to where the Jolley-Rogers' ship was tied.

ARR! Matilda!

...Jim Lad yelled, swinging on a rope.

He landed THUD beside her and said:

Shall we elope?

They skimmed across the ocean, three days beneath the sails.

They sang sea shanties, played 'I spy' and made up pirate tales.

The Jolley-Rogers
dropped their bags and
Jim's mum made some tea.

What a LOVELY view,
and just a ship's length
from the sea!

Matilda, Jim and Nugget went
to Cruncher Club, but amongst the
other pirate kids there
was a big HUBBUB.

Barnacle Bob, the lifeguard,
sat straight and rubbed his eyes.
He thought he'd seen a lubber,
much to his surprise.

But maybe it's a
MERMAID; with this
spyglass I can't see.

I'm sure
I see her swimmin',
in the scurvy sea.

Philippa McCavity was shocked by what she saw.
She was blinded by the sparkles as
Matilda passed her door.

Old Man Grumps was pulling clumps
of hair from out his beard.

My monkey friend
can't find no LICE,
but says her hair
smells very nice!

I ain't seen
nothin' like it.
That little girl
is WEIRD!

I'll mucky up her
gleamin' nails!
My scurvy nail bar
never fails!

Jim's dad's tummy rumbled.
"I need to eat some grub!
I'm feelin' rather peckish,
let's sit outside this pub!"

Do you want
some hard tack?
Shark brains?
Pickled eggs?

Seagull soup?
Dodo burgers?
Battered parrot
legs?

THE WONKY
COMPASS

Matilda turned a little green,
and plumped for pasta bake,
followed by a MASSIVE slice
of crispy weevil cake.

On a nearby table, Betty Bilge was not impressed...

Have ye seen the way that their little girl is dressed?

She dont like maggot-y biscuits!

Or shark brains steeped in brine!

The girl's a fussy eater! She don't eat at all like mine!

She's a bad example, with her knife and fork. If mine learn table MANNERS, all my pirate friends will talk.

I don't think she's a pirate. She's clean and too polite. This ain't the place for LUBBERS, it really isn't right!

Cap'n Day called the Jolley-Rogers to reception.

I've had complaints, but as ye know, it's all about perception.

Are ye sure that she's a pirate? I'm afraid it just won't do, to bring lubbers here to Scurvy Sands; she ain't part of yer crew.

Encourage her to do some stuff to put their minds at rest...

Dig for TREASURE!

Fire a CANNON!

Take the PIRATE TEST!

Reading Mad Jack's map,
Matilda walked ahead.
Jim Lad marched along behind,
listening as she read:

"To the west
of Scurvy Sands,
sank me ship with
all its hands."

"I dragged me treasure chests ashore, where they shall lie for evermore."

"Why we headin' east?" said Jim, "when Mad Jack's map says west?"

"That's just it," Matilda said. "Jack FAILED the pirate test! Using his mirror to check his tattoo, gave him a rather back-to-front view!"

Jim and Tilda dug a hole and soon they heard a CLUNK...

Jim ran to join Matilda.

Is the treasure near?

X marks the spot!

...Matilda said.

We need to dig RIGHT HERE!

They found a hoard of treasure from the ship that sunk,
over two hundred years ago in those days of old,
when Mad Jack McMuddle buried his precious gold.

THANK YOU
for my pirate trip,
I've memories
I'll treasure!

Anytime, Matilda,
it was a scurvy
PLEASURE!

The pirates wailed and
waved goodbye.

Oh, I cannot
help but cry!

They fired their cannons,
flintlocks too,
and watched Matilda
fade from view...

To the EAST of
SCURVY SANDS,
sank me ship with all
its hands. I dragged me
TREASURE CHESTS
ashore, where they WON'T
lie for evermore!

MAD JACK McMUDDLE
Who always got lost and was never
quite sure of which oceans he'd crossed.
'Cause his map-reading skills went often awry,
he'd a compass tattooed above his left eye.

Rats in yer bilges? King chopped off yer hand?
Treasure lost its sparkle?

Then come to
SCURVY SANDS!

Park yer ship
in HERE

Mad Jack's
Water Park

Pedalos